MARC BROWN

Arthur's in Charge

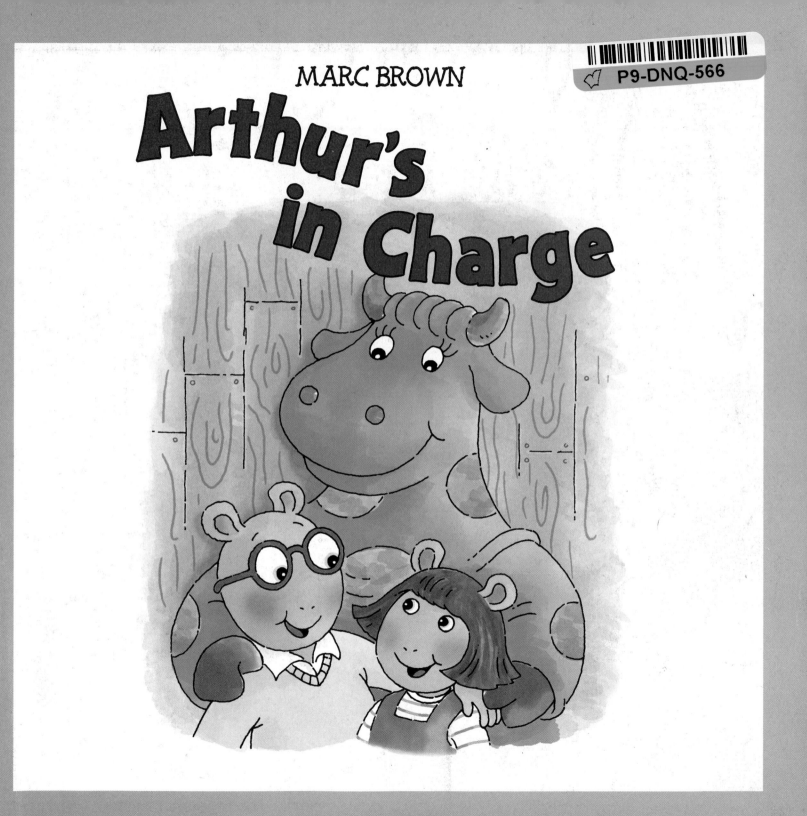

"Mary Moo Cow is coming to the Millcreek Mall today!" shouted D.W.

"Mom!" D.W. begged. "Can I go?"

"I have a hair appointment there later," said Mom. "You can go, but we have to take Arthur with us."

"I need your help," said Mom. "The sooner we go, the faster we'll get home."

"But Mooooooooom!" cried Arthur.

At the mall, Mom said, "You're in charge of D.W.
I'll be right in there."

There was a line of kids waiting to meet
Mary Moo Cow.

"This is going to be a very long day," Arthur sighed.

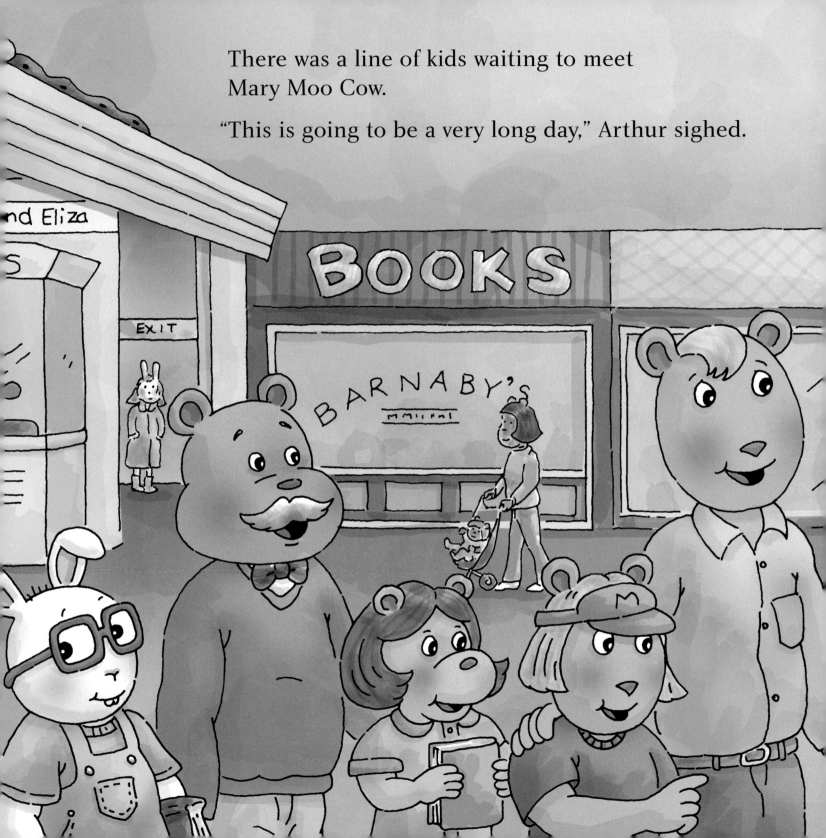

"Will you pose for a picture with Mary Moo Cow and me?" asked D.W.

"Not in a million years," said Arthur.

"Please..." said D.W.

"No way," said Arthur.

CHUCK

Something in the store window caught Arthur's eye. It was the most amazing Bionic Bunny action figure he had ever seen!

"Stay here, D.W.," said Arthur. "I'll be right back."

Arthur stared at the action figure for a long time.

"Wow!" said a familiar voice. It was Buster. "If Bionic Bunny was here, there'd be a *million* kids lined up to see him!"

Suddenly Arthur remembered D.W.

When Arthur and Buster rushed
back to the line, D.W. wasn't there.

They asked if anyone had seen her,
but the kids in line were no help.

"Come on, Buster," said Arthur. "We have to find her."

At Perry's Poodle Pagoda, Arthur and Buster looked around the store. But there was no sign of D.W.

Next, they looked in Dizzy Discs.

Arthur and Buster tried to talk to the sales clerk, but he was too busy dancing to the music.

BEST SELLERS

Then Arthur asked the manager of Barnaby's Books if he'd seen D.W.

"Try the Lost and Found," the manager suggested.

"Thank you!" said Arthur.

Arthur and Buster ran to the Lost and Found.

They saw bowling balls, hula-hoops, teddy bears, but no D.W.

"Have you seen a little girl named D.W. Read?" asked Arthur.

"No, but I'll page her," he said. "Attention please. Will a little lost girl named D.W. Read please come to the Lost and Found."

Suddenly they heard someone shouting, "Arthur!"

It was Arthur's mom. And she wasn't happy.

"You lost D.W.?" she asked.

"I just left her for a second," said Arthur.

"You were supposed to watch her," said Mom.

"I'm sorry, Mom," said Arthur.

"Where did you see her last?" asked Mom.

"In line to meet Mary Moo Cow," said Arthur.

"Let's start there," Mom said.

"Is that a new hairstyle, Mrs. Read?" asked Buster.

When they got to the barnyard, D.W. was not there.

Just then, Arthur heard a familiar giggle coming from the barn. D.W. was inside with Mary Moo Cow!

"D.W., didn't you hear the man call your name?" said Arthur.

"He said 'a lost little girl,' and I wasn't lost," said D.W.

"You should have gone to the Lost and Found," said Arthur.

"He's right," said Mom. "But Arthur, it was *your* responsibility to watch D.W."

"I'm sorry I left you alone, D.W.," said Arthur.

"Look!" said D.W. "I drew a picture of the Bionic Bunny for you."

"Thanks," said Arthur.

D.W. handed her mother the camera.
"Take our picture please," she said.

"What?" said Arthur.

"Say, Moo!" said Mom.

"Very funny!" said Arthur.